BEASTQUEST

THE DARK REALM

→ BOOK SEVENTEEN ←

TUSK
THE MIGHTY MAMMOTH

ADAM BLADE
ILLUSTRATED BY EZRA TUCKER

SCHOLASTIC INC.
New York Toronto London Auckland
Sydney Mexico City New Delhi Hong Kong

With special thanks to Allan Frewin Jones

For Rosie

ISBN 978-0-545-20035-6

Beast Quest series created by Working Partners Ltd., London.
BEAST QUEST is a trademark of Beast Quest Ltd.

Published by Scholastic Inc., 557 Broadway, New York, NY 10012, by arrangement with Working Partners Ltd.
SCHOLASTIC, LITTLE APPLE, and associated logos are trademarks and/or registered trademarks of Scholastic Inc.

12 11 10 9 8 7 6 5 4 3   11 12 13 14 15/0

Designed by Tim Hall
Printed in the U.S.A.   40
First printing, October 2010

Welcome. You stand on the edge of darkness, at the gates of an awful land. This place is Gorgonia, the Dark Realm, where the sky is red, the water black, and Malvel rules. Tom and Elenna — your hero and his companion — must travel here to complete the next Beast Quest.

Gorgonia is home to six most deadly Beasts — Minotaur, Winged Stallion, Sea Monster, Gorgonian Hound, Mighty Mammoth, and Scorpion Man. Nothing can prepare Tom and Elenna for what they are about to face. Their past victories mean little. Only strong hearts and determination will save them now.

Dare you follow Tom's path once more? I advise you to turn back. Heroes can be stubborn and adventures may beckon, but if you decide to stay with Tom, you must be brave and fearless. Anything less will mean certain doom.

Watch your step. . . .

Kerlo the Gatekeeper

"**F**EEL MY BLADE!" MARCO SLASHED AND STABBED with his wooden sword, which was made from a tree branch. "There! I have defeated another enemy of the Gorgon rebels!"

His mother's voice rang out from the nearby settlement. "Marco! Get back on watch!"

With a sigh, Marco crammed his branch sword into his belt and climbed back up the lookout tree, an oak that stood at the edge of the forest. From there he could look down on the small rebel camp where he lived, and see right across the forest, all the way to the northern hills.

The rebel camp was in a heavily forested part of Gorgonia. The leaders of the rebellion came here to make plans for the overthrow of Malvel the Dark Wizard.

Marco's job was very important. If he spotted any Gorgonian guards, his task was to run and warn the Seniors — the men and women who governed the camp. Their weapons would be thrown into a pit and covered by leafy branches, while the leaders would quickly disguise themselves as ordinary hunters and traders.

Marco shifted in his perch. He pulled his tunic close around his neck to ward off the cold wind. A movement caught his eye on a far hilltop. He peered into the distance, but couldn't quite make out what it was. He climbed higher, then gave a gasp of amazement and delight.

It was a huge creature, covered with scales that shimmered. Vast, leathery wings stretched wide, jet-black against the red Gorgonian sky. Puffs of white smoke came from its nostrils.

"A dragon!" Marco murmured. He had never

seen a dragon before, but he loved the stories he had been told of the beautiful, legendary Beasts — and the creature that stood on the far hilltop was most definitely a dragon!

"It's beautiful!" Marco said. But where did it come from? There were no dragons in Gorgonia.

He had to let the Seniors know what he had seen. He was about to climb down the tree when he spotted movement on the far edge of the forest. Trees waved and shuddered, as though something huge was pushing through them.

As he watched, a fearsome creature came stamping out of the forest. It was a mammoth, larger than the biggest house Marco had ever seen. Her back was covered in thick brown hair that hung in shaggy tangles to her feet. The mammoth lifted her head, sending her trunk writhing up into the sky, as she let out a deep battle cry.

Then she thundered up the hillside toward the dragon. Marco could see scars and old wounds on the mammoth's ears — but what he especially noticed were her long, curved tusks. As she charged, they sparkled and glinted like gold.

The dragon turned, lifting its head. Then it opened its wings, preparing to take to the air. But it was too late. Her head down, the mammoth crashed into the dragon's scaly side. She jerked her head up, catching the dragon with her long tusks, heaving the startled Beast onto its side. Marco watched in dismay as the mammoth wrapped her trunk around the dragon's neck and tossed the helpless creature back into the forest.

"No!" Marco shouted.

The mammoth's head lifted sharply. Marco gave a gasp of alarm. The monster had heard him! Small, red eyes peered across the forest, filled with anger and evil. Then she charged through the trees, heading straight for Marco.

The oak shook as the evil Beast's huge head hammered into its trunk. There was a tearing noise as the deep roots were wrenched out of the ground. The tree began to tilt at a dangerous angle. Marco lost his footing and hung by his arms.

But the mammoth had struck the tree with such force that her golden tusks had become embedded in the trunk. She twisted her head, trying to pull herself free. A thick, clear liquid was dripping from the tree. It gave off a terrible, poisonous stench.

The tree was now at such an angle that Marco was able to drop safely to the ground and race back toward his village.

But as he ran, he saw something else that made his heart thud. Marching along the trail was a company of Gorgonian guards. . . .

CHAPTER ONE

TO THE RESCUE!

"TOM!" ELENNA CALLED WITH A SMILE. "IF YOU don't stop playing with your new friend, we'll never get started on our Quest."

Tom grinned back at her. "You'd be doing the same thing if your shadow suddenly came to life!" he said, watching the fleeting black shape as it vanished around the corner of the castle.

His shadow had leaped into action the moment Tom had fitted Kaymon the Gorgon Hound's white diamond into his magic belt.

Tom's vision blurred; then he suddenly realized that he could see two different things at the same time. With his own eyes, he could see the wall of the castle, but he could also see through the shadow's eyes. He was able to scan the land of Gorgonia, stretching away behind the castle.

"So that's my latest magic skill!" Tom gasped. "I'll be able to send my shadow ahead to check for danger. Shadow!" he called. "Come back here, please!"

The shadow bounded back around the corner and skidded to a halt at his feet.

"You're going to make a useful addition to the team!" Tom laughed, as his shadow reattached itself to him. He turned and walked back to where Elenna and his stallion, Storm, were waiting.

Elenna looked questioningly at him. "Do you know where our next Quest will take us?"

Before Tom could reply, the air between them began to ripple like water. Light blazed for a moment and then an image of their friend the Good Wizard Aduro appeared in front of them.

"Is Silver with you?" Elenna asked anxiously.

Her wolf had been badly hurt in their last Quest, and Tartok the Ice Beast had taken him through the gateway into Avantia to be healed.

"He is quite safe," Aduro reassured her. "He is being well looked after. But a new evil Beast awaits you. She is a formidable foe. Her name is Tusk."

"Is she a mammoth?" Tom asked. He had seen the great shaggy animals occasionally in Avantia.

"Yes," Aduro said. "But a mammoth unlike any you have ever imagined."

"What do you mean?" asked Elenna.

The air began to ripple again, and the image of the Good Wizard flickered and trembled. "Alas, I must go," he called, his voice fading. "My magic is weakening. Good luck, my friends — and be careful. You are going into greater danger than you suspect."

The image disappeared.

Tom's heart sank. These brief visits from Aduro always reminded him of how far he was from home. Then he shook himself. *There's no time to waste*, he thought. *A new Quest is waiting for us!*

"At least I know Silver is all right," Elenna said. "Do you think the Gorgonian map will show us where we have to go?"

"I hope so," Tom said. He felt a vibration in his shield. He looked at the six tokens, given to him by the good Beasts of Avantia, that were embedded in it. The scale of Ferno the Fire Dragon was glowing red.

"Ferno is in danger!" Tom said. He took out the map that Malvel had given them. They could never be sure whether it would show them a true path or lead them into deadly peril — but it was the only guide they had.

Spreading out the map, Tom saw a small image of the fire dragon in a region of thick forest.

"That's no more than a day's ride north," Elenna said. She pointed to a red circle drawn on the map on the southern edge of the forest. "And it's close to the rebel camp that Odora marked for us."

"Yes," Tom agreed, remembering the rebel girl who had aided them in their Quest to defeat Narga the Sea Monster. "That's the one thing on this map we *know* we can trust!" He leaped into Storm's saddle. "Come on. We have another good Beast to rescue!"

Elenna sprang up behind him. With a loud neigh, Storm set off at a gallop.

"We'll have to pass close to the rebel camp," Elenna said. "Do you think we should stop there for food and water?"

"That's a good idea," Tom said.

Soon they were moving through a land of rolling hills and forested valleys. Tom looked at his shield. The dragon scale was glowing more darkly now. He had a sense of foreboding as Storm galloped on beneath the red Gorgonian sky. Suddenly, his mind was filled with a dark vision of Ferno writhing and crying out in pain.

"Faster, boy!" Tom urged.

"What's wrong?" Elenna asked, clinging on as the stallion picked up speed.

"I don't think Ferno has long to live," Tom called back. He couldn't keep the concern out of his voice. "I hope we get to him in time!"

Could our Quest be over before it begins? Tom worried to himself.

→ Chapter Two →

Life and Death

THE HILLS AND VALLEYS SPED PAST, BUT Tom could see from the map that they were still some distance from the forest where Ferno was being held.

"Take the reins," he told Elenna, passing them behind his back. "I'll go on ahead. Storm will run faster without my weight."

Without waiting for Storm to stop, Tom jumped out of the saddle. He leaped fearlessly through the air, landing lightly and rolling through the grass. In a moment he was on his feet again. The token from Cypher the Mountain Giant that was embedded in his shield had protected him from the fall.

The magical golden armor that Tom had won in his last Quest was now back in Avantia, and closely guarded in King Hugo's palace, but he had retained the powers it had bestowed upon him. Now the golden leg armor gave him the ability to race ahead of the galloping horse. It was thrilling to be able to run so quickly, feeling the wind in his hair, sensing the trees and boulders flashing by as he sprinted over hills that jutted into the red sky like sunbleached bones. He felt as though he could run forever!

Soon the steep valleys between the hills became more stony, and Tom realized the barren ground was scattered with the skeletons of rotting creatures. The air was filled with the putrid stench of stagnant water. At last he saw the great forest ahead of him. It was a dismal sight, and smelled moldy even from a distance. Tom shivered; it was easy to imagine the hideous creatures that lurked under cover of those gloomy trees.

He looked back and was glad to see that Storm was close behind.

The three companions made their way down the hillside toward the forest.

"This place has an evil feel," Elenna murmured, peering toward the trees. "Tom, look — everything is dead!"

"Not quite everything," Tom said, shuddering as he stared at the great poisonous-looking ferns that climbed up the rotting trees, choking the life out of the blackened, shriveled leaves.

"I recognize those things," Elenna said, her voice trembling. "They're called snake ferns. They grow fast and strangle everything they touch."

Tom nodded. "But Ferno is in here somewhere. We have to go in," he said, pushing his own fears aside. "Come on, we don't have much time."

He stepped under the heavy canopy of branches. The trees were bunched together and the gloomy forest stank of decay. The only things that moved were flabby toads that dripped slime as they hopped among the litter of dead undergrowth.

A dull vibration shook the forest, followed by a heavy boom. Tom stopped, looking at Elenna. Another boom sounded, and then another. The ground trembled and the trees shook around them.

"Footsteps," Tom said, staring into the darkness. "Tusk is near!"

Storm whinnied nervously and stepped back. Tom stroked the frightened horse's neck. "It's all right," he murmured soothingly. "Don't be scared."

Holding the reins, he moved forward again, Elenna close at his side with an arrow in her bow.

"Be careful not to touch the snake ferns," Elenna warned him. "They'll grab you if they get the chance, and once you're caught, there's no getting free again."

Tom nodded and drew his sword. The stink almost made him retch, and the tree trunks that pressed in around them were dripping with a thick, sticky red sap that looked like blood.

They made their way deep into the sinister forest, pushing through large rotting plants. Green light seeped in weakly through the branches. Still the tremors shook the forest.

"We have to get to Ferno," he said. "But how will we ever find him in this dreadful place?"

"You could try calling to him," Elenna suggested.

"Good idea!" Tom declared. "Torgor's ruby will help me understand him." He took a deep breath and placed his hand on the red jewel in his belt. "Ferno!" he called.

Suddenly, his head was filled with the groaning of the trapped dragon.

"I hear him!" he said, his heart aching at the pitiful sound. "He's asking for help."

"Is he saying anything else?" Elenna asked.

Tom frowned, listening hard to the dragon voice

in his head. "There's something about . . . *twin blades*," he said.

"What does that mean?" Elenna asked.

"I don't know," Tom said. "But there's no time to worry about it now." He pointed into the crowded trees. "I'm sure his voice is coming from that direction! Follow me!"

He plunged through the trees, leading Storm and using his sword to sweep aside the huge rotting plants. He was desperate to get to the dragon as quickly as possible.

Then a terrible scream rang out behind him.

"Elenna!" Tom gasped, spinning around. "No!" he shouted as he saw a thick snake fern draw Elenna up into the high branches, its vicious tendrils coiled tight around her ankles!

CHAPTER THREE

AN IMPOSSIBLE CHOICE!

TOM RAN BACK TO WHERE ELENNA WAS HANGING. The long snake fern had reeled her right into the treetops, pulling her up far above his head. She was dangling upside down, squirming and twisting as she tried desperately to get free.

Tom came to a halt beneath her, staring up in alarm.

"Don't worry!" he called up. "I'll get you down! Are you all right?"

"I'm not hurt," Elenna gasped, her face red and her eyes bulging. "The horrible thing took me by surprise, that's all!"

A snake fern spooled down toward Tom like a long, thin tongue, its end twitching. Tom swung his sword at the evil plant, cutting through it. Green sap sprayed out as the fern pulled away from him, writhing as it retreated back into the treetops.

There was no time to lose. "Grab my hands!" he called as he sprang upward, using the power of the magical armor's golden boots to propel him through the air.

He managed to catch hold of her hands, but almost immediately, Elenna let out a piercing yell. "It's not going to work," she cried. "The ferns are tightening around my legs! They won't let go!"

Tom hung from her grip, watching in dismay as a long tendril of snake fern came creeping down Elenna's body and coiled itself around her neck.

He swung himself, desperately hoping that their

combined weight would rip Elenna loose from the ferns.

"Tom, don't!" Elenna choked as the fern tightened around her neck. "It's strangling me! Let go, please!"

Reluctantly, Tom released Elenna's hands and dropped to the ground. Elenna brought her hands up to her throat and forced her fingers under the tightening fern, pulling at it and gasping for breath.

Tom stared up at her. What could he do now? Even with the power of the magic boots, he couldn't leap high enough to cut through the ferns that were holding her.

The heavy footsteps were still booming through the forest, making the ground shake. And Ferno's voice was still calling weakly in Tom's head. He had to think quickly.

"I'll throw you my sword," Tom called up to Elenna. "Then you can cut the ferns!"

"No," gasped Elenna. "If I let go of the fern around my neck, it'll choke me before I can cut myself free. I'm all right for the moment. Go and save Ferno!"

Tom hated the thought of leaving Elenna in such danger. If only Silver were here, he could send the loyal wolf in search of Ferno while he helped his friend.

As Tom hesitated, the dragon's voice grew louder in his mind and the booming footsteps shook the trees around him.

"The footsteps are getting closer," Elenna called down. "Tom, go and find Ferno — quickly!"

"I'll be back as soon as possible!" called Tom. "Hold on, Elenna. Come on, boy!" He leaped into Storm's saddle and urged the brave horse into the trees, toward the cries of the dragon.

Tom kept his sword ready, hacking and slashing at any ferns that came too close. The ferns moved away from him as he rode through the thick trees, and then closed in again behind him. Tom knew that without his sword, the ferns would have swarmed over him by now.

Finally he saw Ferno through the trees. The great dragon was huddled against a tree, snake ferns coiled all around his body so that he could hardly move. He looked exhausted. The evil tendrils were tearing at his scales and twisting around his limbs and wings. But at least he was alive!

Ferno lifted his head as he caught sight of Tom, and feeble puffs of gray smoke bubbled from his nostrils.

"He can't breathe fire," Tom gasped. The good Beast was helpless.

"I'll save you," he shouted, brandishing his sword. "Come on, Storm!"

The stallion neighed and plunged forward. Soon Tom's bright blade would be hacking through those deadly ferns and Ferno would be free!

Then a vast shape came smashing out of the

trees to their left. At first, all Tom saw were flying branches and whole trees uprooted and thrown through the air. Then, lunging through the chaos, came the most immense Beast Tom had ever seen.

Tusk came thundering forward, her huge trunk lifted as she roared, her feet crushing everything in her path.

The evil Beast was heading directly toward them!

⇥ Chapter Four ⇤

Beaten!

Tusk's broad, shaggy back was as high as the tallest trees. Her trunk rose up over the branches like a monstrous snake ready to strike. The thick gray skin of her head was laced with old battle scars, and her huge ears were torn and ragged at the edges.

When she opened her mouth to roar, the air was filled with the stench of her breath. Tom found himself staring in terror down a great red throat, wide enough to swallow him whole. But most fearsome of all were the long, curved, golden tusks, their sides scored with deep scratches, their points razor-sharp. Now he understood what Ferno had meant by *twin blades*. A thick, slimy liquid dripped from the tusks. It stank horribly!

The mighty monster rushed toward Tom, an evil glint in her eyes. He had time only to raise his shield in defense before she was upon him.

Storm reared up, neighing in fear, and lurched to one side. Tom gasped with relief as the mammoth's head went past them, her trunk rearing up as she bellowed in rage. Then his stomach dropped as he felt himself slip out of the saddle.

"No!" Tom cried. He threw out his hands to break his fall and felt the skin being scraped off his palms as he crashed through the dead plants. The force of the fall drove all the air out of his lungs and he lay gasping on the forest floor, his ears ringing and his bones jarred. Only the power of the golden armor had protected him from serious injury!

Storm was bucking and rearing, neighing furiously and kicking out with his hooves. Tom could see

Ferno struggling uselessly, caught tight by the ferns. The dragon's angry voice filled his head.

Tusk ignored the horse and the dragon, turning instead to fix her red eyes on Tom. He scrambled to his feet, backing away through the trees, his shield up, his sword in his fist.

"Come on! I'm ready for you!" he shouted.

The mammoth stomped toward him, her golden tusks tearing through the trees. But even as Tom struggled to think of a way to fight the Beast, he noticed an amber jewel embedded in one of the tusks. Another token for his magic belt!

But how was he going to triumph over this tremendous Beast?

Then a familiar mocking laugh echoed through the stifling air of the forest.

"Malvel!" Tom hissed, staring around for some sign of the Dark Wizard.

"You will never defeat Tusk," said the cruel, cold voice. "She will crush you like an insect!"

Anger flared through Tom. He brandished his sword and shouted, "While there is blood in my veins, I will defeat every Beast you send!"

Malvel's laughter filled his ears, but Tom wasn't going to turn back from his battle.

Tusk was standing in an area of crushed trees, watching Tom with her evil eyes. Storm stood to one side, pawing the ground anxiously.

Tom sprang toward the mammoth, leaping high, his sword whirling. The power of the golden boots sent him soaring above the tusks and he landed high on the mammoth's trunk.

Tusk roared in fury, but before she had the chance to shake him loose, he jumped again, this time landing on her head. He dropped to his knees, one hand clutching at the Beast's coarse hair to help him balance. He stared in astonishment at the deep scars that cut into the monster's thick hide. How many battles had this huge creature fought and won?

I have to end this fight quickly! Tom thought. Was his sword strong enough to pierce her skull?

He lifted his blade, ready to plunge it down into the Beast's head.

But Tusk was too quick for him. Her trunk came sweeping back, as thick as a log. Tom ducked, but the trunk smashed into his shoulder and knocked him onto his back. Before he could regain his footing, Tusk shook her head, trying to throw him off.

"I won't let you!" Tom cried. He clung grimly to the Beast's ear, desperate not to fall under those pounding feet. He could see Ferno letting out cries of distress and struggling wildly in the loops of snake fern. The good dragon was trying to come to his aid.

Suddenly, Storm ran forward, rearing up on his hind legs and beating at the mammoth's sides with his hooves. But it was hopeless — Tusk seemed to hardly notice Storm's blows. Then the Beast reared up high above the trees, swinging her great head in a final effort to throw Tom loose. Her enraged roaring shook the forest.

Tom felt his grip weakening. He scrambled with his feet, but couldn't find a foothold. Tusk came thundering down onto all fours. The shock of the impact broke Tom's hold and he fell to the ground.

He looked up, horror-struck. The great feet of Tusk were rearing up again, ready to crush him to death!

Chapter Five

Poison!

At the last moment, Tom rolled aside, the blood pulsing in his temples.

"I won't give up!" he gasped.

He heard Elenna's voice calling from across the forest. "Tom! Are you all right?"

"Yes!" he shouted back.

Storm was still neighing wildly, and beating at the mighty mammoth with his hooves.

Using the power of the golden boots, Tom sprang up once more and regained his footing on the evil Beast's great head. Ferno let out a delighted roar and Tom turned to see the trapped dragon struggling even more fiercely against his bonds.

"Come on, Ferno!" Tom urged the good Beast. "You can do it!"

Tusk gave a bellow of anger. Then she turned from the dragon, and went lumbering off through the trees with Tom still clinging grimly to her head.

Tom was being taken away from his Quest!

But Storm came galloping after them, foam at his lips and his eyes blazing as he chased the great mammoth through the trees.

As Tusk thundered along, Tom had to duck in order to avoid the falling branches and flying splinters of smashed trees.

He soon realized that the mammoth was approaching the place where the snake ferns held Elenna captive.

Gripping the coarse hair on the Beast's head, Tom stared forward. Yes! He could see Elenna now. The snake ferns still held her tightly in their deadly grip.

Elenna twisted around to look at Tom. "Hold on tight!" she shouted.

Tusk came to a halt, her great feet pounding the earth as she peered through the trees. She had heard Elenna's voice. Her trunk went up and she let out an earsplitting bellow as her red eyes caught sight of Elenna dangling upside down in the treetops. The mammoth moved toward her, ripping up trees with her trunk as she went.

Tom had to do something!

Getting carefully to his feet, Tom balanced himself on the great swaying head. He had one hope of saving Elenna. He swung his arm back and sent his sword spinning through the air. The blade sliced through the ferns that were holding her. But it was not enough! One thick tendril still gripped her by the ankle.

Tom watched as his sword struck a tree and went tumbling to the ground. *I've lost my weapon, and Elenna's still not free!* he thought desperately. He snatched hold of Tusk's left ear and wrenched at it with all his might, trying to force her to turn aside. But even using every ounce of his strength, Tom couldn't turn the evil Beast. Then Tusk's trunk came swinging back toward him.

It struck him with another vicious blow, sweeping his legs out from under him and sending him plunging to the forest floor.

Dazed and gasping for breath, Tom saw Elenna struggling wildly. Her face was bright red from being held upside down for so long. He staggered to his feet and ran after Tusk, desperate to help his friend. Storm came racing up, and Tom leaped into the saddle, shouting at the top of his voice, "Tusk! Leave her! It's me you want!"

But the evil Beast ignored him. Tusk's long trunk reached out for Elenna, but before it was able to grab her, Elenna tore frantically through the final green tendril and plunged through the air. As she fell she knocked her arm against one of the mammoth's jagged tusks. Its gleaming point pierced her skin and Tom saw red blood appear.

"No!" Tom shouted, as she landed with a thump on the forest floor and lay still. He jumped from Storm's back and bounded forward, snatching up his sword from where it had fallen. He ran in close to Tusk's hind leg and drove the point of the blade deep into the mammoth's foot.

Tusk let out a bellow of pain that shook the ground.

Tom wrenched the sword out and thrust it in again, seeing thick red blood spurt from the wounds.

The mammoth reared up, roaring with anger as the sword dug deep into her flesh, then pulled away, her head twisting around and her trunk crashing through the trees.

But Tom was too quick for her. He bounded away through the forest, running in a curve that took him to where Elenna had fallen.

He pulled her under the cover of some thick bushes.

"Thank you," Elenna whispered weakly.

"We're not safe yet," Tom said, looking anxiously at her. He quickly examined the wound on her arm. He could see that it was infected. The liquid that dripped from the evil Beast's tusks must be poisonous!

He had to do something to help Elenna. But what?

CHAPTER SIX

ESCAPE INTO DANGER!

With a surge of hope, Tom remembered the rebel camp near the forest's edge. Surely someone there would be able to help?

But he had to act quickly. Tusk was close by, still bellowing with pain. He knew that at any moment those evil eyes might turn toward them.

"Can you walk?" he asked Elenna.

She struggled feebly to get to her feet. "No," she groaned. "My legs have gone numb!"

"Don't worry," Tom said. "I'll carry you. We're going to the rebel camp."

"It's too far," Elenna gasped. "You'll never manage it."

A fearsome roar blasted through the forest, and the hammering of huge feet shook the ground.

"Tusk is coming!" Tom gasped. How would they get away in time?

Then the sound of hoofbeats came echoing through the trees. Tom looked up — Storm had found them!

"Good boy!" Tom called as the stallion came to a halt at their side. "Stay with Elenna. I'll see to Tusk!"

Tom stepped out into the path of the mammoth, his sword raised high. The evil Beast was bellowing with frustration and pain, her trunk swishing, her eyes blazing like furnaces. Blood oozed from her injured foot.

Tom ran in close, striking at her poisoned tusks with his sword. The blade cut deep scores in them. Tusk raised her trunk, preparing to bring it down on him in a killing blow.

"You'll never catch me!" Tom shouted as he dashed toward a patch of dense snake ferns. At the last moment, he leaped into the air. Tusk lumbered after him, but became entangled in the mass of fern. As she tried to pull herself clear, more and more ferns came snaking down toward her, coiling around her tusks, gripping her trunk, reaching for her head and body.

"It worked!" Tom panted as he landed again. The more Tusk pulled and strained, the more tightly the ferns wrapped themselves around her.

He ran back to where Elenna and Storm were waiting. Gently lifting Elenna in his arms, he placed her on Storm's back.

"Hold on tight," he told her, pushing back a lock of hair from her pale face. Elenna smiled weakly and nodded. "Storm — follow me!" he ordered, turning away. *Elenna mustn't see that I'm worried about her*, he thought.

Tom ran through the trees, Storm close behind. The forest rang to the sound of Tusk's furious bellowing. Tom knew it was only a matter of time before she broke free and thundered after them.

They came out of the forest and Tom saw the rebel camp ahead of them with its high fence of sharpened wooden stakes. He brought Storm to a halt and lifted Elenna down from the saddle. Her face was gray and she was shivering all over.

"Elenna?" he murmured. Although her eyes were open, they were glazed and blank. The poison was working fast!

Tom took Epos's feather from his shield. It had the ability to heal all wounds. He touched it to her swollen arm. Elenna groaned but nothing happened.

"This Gorgonian poison must be too strong," he whispered. He left Elenna resting against a tree, with Storm watching over her. Then he ran toward the camp. The gates were shut and there was no sign of life.

"Hello!" he called, hammering desperately on the gates. "I need help!"

He knew he was putting the rebels in danger by shouting out like that and drawing attention to their camp, but he had no choice. He had to save Elenna!

No one answered. Was the camp deserted? Had the rebels fled?

He stared up anxiously at the tall gates. There was no way he could climb over them. How was he ever going to get into the camp?

I'll send in my shadow, thought Tom. *He'll find out what's happening in there.*

Tom felt a curious sensation in his feet as his shadow peeled itself free, scaled the fence, and dropped out of sight. Soon he began to see through the shadow's eyes as it wove between the huts. Where was everyone?

Then the shadow peered out from behind a hut. Tom's breath hissed through his teeth. Now he

could understand why no one had answered his calls.

All the rebels had been lined up in an open space in the middle of the camp. Armed Gorgonian guards were watching over them, while more guards ransacked the huts, searching for weapons.

Tom's heart quickened as he saw the tall, thin boy who was in command. It was Seth! Tom had encountered this boy before in previous Quests; he was one of Malvel's most trusted followers.

At that moment one of the guards shouted and pointed. He had seen the shadow! Seth spun around, his blue eyes blazing.

"Capture it!" Seth shouted. "Don't let it escape!"

"Come back!" Tom whispered urgently. The shadow turned and ran. A few moments later the wooden gates of the camp were flung open and a troop of guards came running out, carrying swords.

His plan had gone horribly wrong. Instead of

helping Elenna, he had led them into another perilous situation. He had to get his friend to safety. He turned to run back to Elenna and Storm — but found he couldn't lift his feet. No matter how hard he tried, his feet remained glued to the ground.

His shadow must be too far away! It had to be part of the magic. So long as he was separated from it, he was helpless!

Chapter Seven

An Old Enemy

Seth ran ahead of the guards, drawing his sword and coming toward Tom with an evil smile. Tom struggled hard, but he still couldn't move.

Seth was a good swordsman. Tom knew he would not survive if he could not move, no matter how desperately he tried to twist his body to defend himself.

But then Tom's shadow came leaping and bounding through the grass. For a moment, Seth and the shadow were neck and neck, only ten paces away from where Tom stood frozen.

"Come on!" Tom urged.

His shadow gave one final burst, springing ahead of Seth. It gave a twisting leap into the air and landed at Tom's feet.

Tom turned on his heel and bounded to the side just in time, avoiding Seth's blade as it sliced the air at his throat. Snarling with rage, Seth lifted his sword high and brought it slashing down toward Tom's head. Instinctively, Tom lifted his shield to block the attack, then dug his heels into the ground and thrust out with his shield, throwing Seth's blade to one side. Then Tom brought his own sword up, aiming for Seth's evil heart!

But Seth was too quick to be caught out easily. He danced aside, knocking Tom's sword away and then spinning around with his sword held out in both hands, the sharp blade slicing toward Tom's neck.

Tom ducked as the razor-edged blade bit the air above his head. He hoped that the miss would have thrown Seth off balance, but as Tom moved in, Seth leaped out of reach.

They glared at each other.

"I will enjoy killing you!" Seth snarled.

"I feel sorry for you if killing gives you pleasure," Tom retorted angrily. "But I will never be your victim!"

Seth lifted his sword high and charged at Tom, howling in anger and hatred.

Tom stood firm, gripping his sword and raising it as Seth brought his blade down. The two swords clashed, the impact numbing Tom's arms and jarring his shoulders.

They were face-to-face. Tom looked into Seth's furious pale eyes. The boy's mouth twisted in an ugly grimace as he used all his strength to try to force Tom's sword back.

But Tom was not afraid. Grunting with effort, he hammered his shield into Seth's body, following through with a stab to Seth's chest.

But Seth knocked the sword aside and stepped forward, his blade swinging. Tom leaped back just in time to avoid a swipe that would have taken his head off his shoulders.

The Gorgonian guards were moving toward them, swords up and ready.

"Keep back!" Seth shouted to his men. "He's mine!"

Tom smiled grimly; at least he wasn't being overwhelmed by the guards. But if he defeated Seth, Tom knew that they would be ready to attack.

He glanced over his shoulder. Elenna was lying in the grass with Storm standing over her. The noble stallion was tossing his head and whinnying as he saw his master in danger. But Storm would not leave Elenna's side unless Tom called him. If only Silver were with them! He might have been able to help defend Seth's attack.

Seth charged once more, beating Tom back. Blow after blow clanged on his shield as he fought to hold his ground. Every thrust and lunge by Tom was fended off by Seth. How long could Tom survive?

Then Tom spotted something that lifted his spirits. The rebels were pouring from the gates, armed with bows and arrows. Seth's men had left the rebels unguarded — and now they were about to pay the price for their carelessness.

"Surrender now!" Tom snarled at Seth.

The evil boy's eyes glittered with malice. "Never," he hissed. "Throw down your sword before I cut you up!"

There was an echoing twang as every rebel loosed his bowstring. Suddenly, the red Gorgonian sky was thick with black arrows.

Seth spun around, staring in alarm at the speeding arrows.

"Stop the archers!" he howled to his men. "Attack them!" But the guards were thrown into panic as the arrows rained down upon their armor.

Tom knew he had to make the most of the rebel attack. He raced to where Elenna lay helpless in the grass, lifted her limp body into the saddle, and led Storm under the cover of the forest.

"We need to get away from those guards," he muttered, as he squatted behind a thick tree trunk.

A second volley of arrows darkened the sky. The guards were racing about in terror.

Seth took a few steps toward the forest, searching for Tom among the trees. But then he looked over his shoulder — if he did not act quickly, his men would be mowed down by those flying arrows!

He shouted a final curse at Tom, then ran back toward his men. "Guards of Gorgonia," he shouted. "Follow me!"

He ran away from the camp, his men following as the arrows hissed through the air around their ears.

"We will meet again!" Seth howled to Tom. "And on that day, you will die!"

There was cheering from the rebels as the Gorgonian guards fled. A few of the rebels came running toward them. Tom recognized one of them, a small, slender figure racing ahead of the others.

It was Odora, the rebel girl who had helped them in their fight against Narga the Sea Monster. She must have joined up with the other rebels at the camp. Tom left his friends to emerge from the cover of the trees and meet her.

"Elenna is hurt," Tom said, coming to a panting halt. There wasn't any time to say anything else in greeting.

"What has happened to her?" Odora gasped.

At that moment the forest shook with the roaring of the enraged Tusk.

"She was cut by the tusk of a huge mammoth," Tom explained. "The wound is poisoned."

"Do not fear," Odora said. "There is a medicine woman in the camp. Help me carry her there!"

"But I can't come with you." He turned, staring through the thick trees. "I have to go back and face the evil Beast who did this, and I have to rescue another good friend!"

More of the rebels had arrived by now.

"Go," said Odora, nodding her head in understanding. "Do what you have to do. We'll take Elenna to the camp."

Tom led them to where Elenna and Storm were waiting. One of the men took Storm's reins and began to lead him out of the forest, Elenna's body draped across the stallion's neck.

Tom knew he could trust Odora and the rebels. He only hoped they could help Elenna before the poison did its worst.

He watched them return to the camp. Then he turned and walked into the forest.

Did he have the strength to fight Tusk alone?

CHAPTER EIGHT

NEW ALLIES

TOM PUSHED HIS WAY THROUGH THE TREES. HE could hear the roaring of the evil Beast, and feel the ground trembling from the pounding of her massive feet. Although he could not see her, he knew she must have broken free from the snake ferns. He pressed on, heading deeper into the forest.

Dread filled him, but he didn't hesitate; his destiny lay ahead of him and he marched on through the trees to meet it.

After a while, a sound behind him made him freeze. He peered into the trees. Someone was there!

"Show yourself!" he commanded.

Odora stepped out of the shadows. At her back were twenty or more men and women from the rebel camp. Tom saw that some were armed with swords and bows, but others carried only simple weapons — pitchforks, axes, and sticks. Many of them carried long coils of rope over their shoulders, weighted at one end with fierce grappling hooks.

"We want to help you," Odora said. "Most of our people have stayed behind to guard the camp, but we couldn't let you fight the great mammoth alone. We want to defeat Malvel's power, too."

Tom smiled. "Thank you," he said. "Come on — as quietly as you can."

He strode ahead with Odora beside him and the others following. The roaring of the mammoth grew gradually louder and Tom could see trees thrashing about. She was close now!

Now that he was deep into the forest, he could hear the plaintive cries of the captured dragon.

Tom sent his thoughts out to the good Beast.

While there is blood in my veins, I will not let you die! He could tell that his words gave comfort to Ferno.

He waited until all the rebels were gathered around him. "We must split into two groups," he explained. "We need to strike Tusk from both sides at once. Use your ropes to try to bring her down — but make sure that you avoid her poisonous tusks!"

Tom put Odora in charge of one group of rebels, and led the other group himself. They split up and went creeping through the trees.

Finally, they saw Tusk! She was roaring and stamping among the crushed trees. Torn vines trailed from her limbs and hung over her broad back. Tom could see that she was too engrossed in her battle against the snake ferns to spot the people creeping toward her.

Tom gestured to Odora. She waved back and a few seconds later the two groups of rebels flooded into the open space.

Tusk bellowed as she finally caught sight of her attackers, her golden tusks glinting dangerously in the sunlight.

You're too late! Tom thought, hope surging through him. "Use your ropes!" he shouted as the rebels came in close to the huge Beast.

Rope after rope went snaking up, the hooks digging into the monster's flesh.

"Climb up onto her back!" shouted Odora.

Rebels swung up on the ropes, attacking Tusk with swords and pitchforks.

"Use your bows!" came another shout.

Arrows were fired, but they sprang back off her thick hide. Axes pounded the Beast, but Tusk hardly seemed to feel the blows as she shook rebels off her back and threatened to trample others underfoot.

"She's too strong!" wailed one man. "We'll never beat her!"

"Yes, we will!" Tom shouted. "Don't despair!"

He moved in toward the Beast's great head, watching those poisonous tusks. He hoped that the attack would confuse Tusk enough so that he would be able to get in close and deliver a killing thrust to the creature's throat.

But Tusk was not so easily beaten! She thrashed about, the ropes coming loose and the rebels swinging helplessly from her back.

A cold, cruel voice sounded in Tom's ears. It was Malvel, returning to taunt him. "You will never defeat me!" he whispered.

"I will always defeat you!" Tom shouted back, springing toward Tusk's head. He hacked at the mammoth's tusks, trying to get in close enough to stab her. But no matter how hard he fought, he could not get past the tusks and the swiping trunk. He saw the light of triumph glittering in the mammoth's eyes.

The rebels were falling back now, their weapons

useless against the mighty Beast. A blow from her trunk sent Tom sprawling, his sword slipping from his fingers. Tusk seemed as powerful as ever.

Tom struggled to his feet, his shield up to ward off another crushing blow. If only Elenna were there with him! Without his friend it was as if half his strength and determination were missing.

Another blow from the mighty trunk knocked him to his knees. The rebels were doing their best, but their weapons had no magic, and the arrows, pitchforks, and sticks were bouncing uselessly off Tusk's hide.

He heard Malvel laughing at him. He had failed. All was lost!

But then, as Tusk raised a mighty foot ready to crush the life out of him, Tom saw a slender figure come riding through the trees on a stallion.

It was Elenna and Storm!

CHAPTER NINE

BATTLE TO THE DEATH!

AN ARROW FLEW FROM ELENNA'S BOW. THE shaft sank deep into Tusk's forefoot and the great Beast reared back, her ferocious red eyes glittering as a second arrow cut through the air, striking her other front foot.

Tusk backed away, her roars changing to bellows of agony as she tried to pull the arrows from her feet with her trunk. But her trunk was too big to grip the arrows, and all she did was drive the shafts deeper into the tender flesh of her feet.

Tom brandished his sword and called to the rebels, "Attack!"

Odora let out a battle cry and leaped toward the mammoth. The other rebels joined in, hurling weapons and slashing at her hide. The huge monster stumbled back through the trees, her vicious, poison-dripping tusks gleaming.

Storm cantered up to Tom. Elenna looked down at him, her eyes shining.

"You're better!" Tom said in amazement.

"The medicine woman had an antidote to the poison," she said. "I feel fine. Come on, let's finish the job!"

Tom ran alongside Storm as they joined the attack on the retreating mammoth.

The rebels were all around the Beast now, some with scarves across their faces to protect them from the horrible stench of her matted hair. They stabbed at her feet with their pitchforks and swords, driving her deeper into the forest.

Above Tusk's roars, Tom could hear Ferno's mournful voice in his head. The dragon was very weak; his struggles against the snake ferns had drained all his strength.

But as Tusk retreated, Tom realized that she was moving toward the place where Ferno lay imprisoned.

Tom leaped in close to the Beast's head, thrusting with his sword, dancing aside as the cruel tusks swept through the air and the trunk hammered into the ground. He stabbed at her feet once more, cutting bloody wounds, driving the Beast as she tried to escape his darting blade.

In her agony, she lifted herself up on her back legs. She towered over them, filling the sky. Then she staggered, unable to keep her balance. For a terrible moment, Tom thought she was going to crash down on top of him. But one back leg buckled under her and she toppled onto her side, smashing trees to splinters and rocking the ground as she fell.

As the trees were torn down, Tom saw that Ferno was lying close by, still struggling among the ferns, his wings flapping exhaustedly. The mammoth fought to get up, but as she did so her tusks tore through the snake ferns that held the dragon, ripping them to shreds.

"The ropes!" Tom shouted to the rebels. "Tie Tusk down while she's still on the ground!"

Ropes coiled over Tusk's high side, the grappling hooks digging in as the rebels fought to prevent the evil Beast from getting to her feet.

Tom leaped through the air, using the magic of his golden boots once more, and landed on Tusk's neck. He caught hold of her ear, and he twisted her huge head so that her tusks pierced the ground.

"You will do no more harm with your poison!" Tom shouted, and jumped off her head, swinging his sword. The blade cut cleanly through one of the tusks. The mammoth's bellow was deafening, but Tom swung his sword again. As he chopped off the second tusk, the entire bulk of the Beast glowed with a blazing green light.

Tom covered his eyes as the glow exploded through the forest, and when he looked up again, the mammoth was gone. In her place was a radiant emerald archway.

"It's Avantia!" Elenna cried, leaping from the saddle and running to Tom's side. She was right — through the archway, the beautiful rolling hills of Avantia could clearly be seen under a blue sky.

A joyful roar rang out. It was Ferno, rising up out of the shreds of snake fern, his black wings spreading magnificently, a burst of fire jetting from his nostrils.

"He's free!" Elenna cried. "He can go back to Avantia now!"

Tom wiped his brow. He turned and saw the Gorgonian rebels gazing spellbound through the arch. Tom suddenly had an idea. *I can help these people*, he thought.

"This gateway will take you to freedom," he called. "But you must go now — the gate will only be open for a short time."

Odora stepped forward. "But what about the rest of our companions — the other rebels?"

"There's no time to gather them," Tom explained. "It's now or never!"

Odora nodded. She gave Tom and Elenna a quick hug, then beckoned to her friends. They gazed at one another for a moment or two, hesitating, then followed Odora through the arch.

Tom turned to Elenna. "I could never have defeated Tusk without you!" he said.

Elenna nodded, smiling. "We're quite a team!"

But her smile faded as she looked at something over Tom's shoulder. He turned.

Kerlo the Gatekeeper was standing under the trees, watching them.

"I wondered when you would come," Tom called, as the one-eyed gatekeeper strode forward with his cane in his hand.

But Kerlo's face was grim.

A cold fear filled Tom's heart — something was terribly wrong!

CHAPTER TEN

THE GATEKEEPER'S WARNING

TOM GAZED UNEASILY AT THE TALL GATEKEEPER as he leaned on his cane. The light of the emerald arch was reflected in his one good eye.

"Was that wise?" asked the old man.

"How can you ask?" Tom said. "The rebels are fighting against Malvel. They're good people — they deserve to find a better life!"

"Good people?" Kerlo rumbled. "Are you sure? What if they do not wish to be ruled by King Hugo? What will happen to Avantia then?"

Tom stared through the shimmering emerald arch, but Odora and the rebels had already moved out of sight. Surely Kerlo was mistaken. The rebels would not cause problems in Avantia — would they?

Tom turned back to the gatekeeper, but the ragged man had vanished back into the shadows of the forest.

"Don't let him worry you," Elenna said. "You've done well. You've liberated Ferno and you've destroyed another of Malvel's evil Beasts. Aduro would be proud of you."

Tom nodded, but he still felt uneasy. A delighted roar from Ferno interrupted his thoughts. The dragon came toward them, his bright eyes shining with pleasure, his scales glossy and shining once more. He lifted his long snout and let out a burst of flame that lit up the gloomy sky. Evening was approaching, and the red Gorgonian sky was darkening rapidly. The sparkling emerald arch was glowing even more brightly in the gathering gloom, but Tom knew it would fade soon.

"You must go home now, Ferno!" Tom called to the dragon.

Ferno flapped his wings and gave another happy roar. Then he bowed his head in thanks to the two friends before flying through the emerald gateway. There was a final swish of his tail and then he was gone.

"Another Quest completed," said Elenna.

Tom nodded. "But I'd like to get out of this forest before night falls," he said.

Storm whinnied in agreement. None of them wanted to spend the night near the deadly snake ferns! Tom took the reins and the three companions walked through the trees, heading for the rebel camp.

A sound at their backs brought them to a halt. Tom drew his sword and Elenna put an arrow to the string of her bow. They waited in uneasy silence as something drew closer.

A gray shape sprang out of the darkness.

"Silver!" cried Elenna, dropping her bow as her beloved wolf came leaping toward them. He almost knocked her off her feet as he bounded around her, wagging his tail, his eyes gleaming. It looked as though his stay in Avantia had restored him to full health. Tom laughed and Storm let out a neigh of pleasure. The four friends were united once more!

Then Silver padded over to Tom and dropped something from his mouth. It lay shining on the ground — an amber jewel!

Tom picked it up. "It's from the mammoth's tusk," he said. "Thank you, Silver."

He slipped the jewel into place on his magic belt. Immediately he felt a new power flowing through him. He turned to Elenna.

"The amber jewel is working!" he told her. "It will help me to be a better fighter — my battle skills already feel so much sharper!"

His body filled with renewed strength, Tom threw his sword high in the air and caught it with a shout. "I pity the next Beast that tries to stop us!" he laughed. "Let's get out of here — I'm sure there will be food and beds at the rebel camp!"

But as they stepped out of the forest, Tom could not shake off memories of the gatekeeper's warning.

What was waiting for him back in Avantia? He'd find out soon enough. But first, there was another evil Beast to defeat.